Advance praise for *Living With Viola*

"Beautifully illustrated, relatable, and genuine."
–Molly Brooks, creator of *Sanity & Tallulah*

"Heartfelt and fun, *Living With Viola* is
going to mean a lot to an awful lot of kids."
–Eleanor Davis, creator of *Stinky* and *You & a Bike & a Road*

"*Living With Viola* is told with both compassion and humor.
Livy is a character with whom many readers will identify, and
even more will empathize, as they accompany her on her
journey through school, friendship, and family. Delightful."
–Lisa Brown, creator of *The Phantom Twin*

"How does one exist when everything appears to be against
us, especially ourselves? Through this beautifully drawn,
and at turns funny and heart-wrenching story, Livy finds her
way. Rosena Fung's deeply moving and empowering book
is sure to enter the kids' Graphic Medicine canon."
–Fiona Smyth, creator of *Sex Is A Funny Word*
(with Cory Silverberg) and *Somnambulance*

"*Living With Viola* is an explosion of colors and emotions
Rosena Fung has artfully woven into a heartbreakingly
familiar tale many of her readers will feel in their bones. I'll
be tucking this important read onto my bookshelf to share
with my own child so she can see how words can wound,
even, maybe especially, when you turn them on yourself."
–Britt Wilson, author of *Ghost Queen*
and *Cat Dad, King of the Goblins*

"*Living With Viola* . . . fearlessly takes young readers
into the darkness of Livy's panic, anxiety, fear, and sense
of being alone but, like the allies that Livy will find, is also
there to guide them back into the light. One of the best
debuts I have ever seen."
–Jeffrey Canton, children's book
columnist for *The Globe and Mail*

To Mark, for your love,
and Mom and Dad, for your sacrifice.
—R.F.

© 2021 Rosena Fung (text and illustrations)

Cover art by Rosena Fung, designed by Rosena Fung and Paul Covello
Interior designed by Rosena Fung and Paul Covello
Edited by Serah-Marie McMahon
Copyedited by Mary Ann Blair
Proofread by Doeun Rivendell
Expert read/Cantonese language review by Ambrose Li

If you or someone you know is dealing with anxiety, panic, or any other mental health issues, know that you are not alone. In addition to confiding in a trusted adult, you can find support in Canada through Kids Help Phone at kidshelpphone.ca or by calling 1-800-668-6868. For Canada and the US, you can find support through the Crisis Text Line at crisistextline.org or by texting 741741. Both resources will connect you to trained counselors.

Annick Press Ltd.

We acknowledge the support of the Canada Council for the Arts and the Ontario Arts Council, and the participation of the Government of Canada/la participation du gouvernement du Canada for our publishing activities.

Library and Archives Canada Cataloguing in Publication

Title: Living with Viola / Rosena Fung.
Names: Fung, Rosena, author.
Identifiers: Canadiana (print) 20210188596 | Canadiana (ebook) 20210188618 | ISBN 9781773215488 (hardcover) | ISBN 9781773215495 (softcover) | ISBN 9781773215518 (PDF) | ISBN 9781773215501 (HTML)
Subjects: LCGFT: Graphic novels.
Classification: LCC PN6733.F86 L58 2021 | DDC j741.5/971—dc23

Published in the U.S.A. by Annick Press (U.S.) Ltd.
Distributed in Canada by University of Toronto Press.
Distributed in the U.S.A. by Publishers Group West.

Printed in China

annickpress.com
rosenafung.com

Also available as an e-book. Please visit annickpress.com/ebooks for more details.

LIVING
WITH
VIOLA

ROSENA FUNG

annick
press
toronto • berkeley

5

8

9

*IN CANTONESE

21

27

33

35

43

44

46

49

50

51

54

60

63

FFFT
GIRLS CAN'T BE MVP!!

CAN TOO!

YOU'RE GOOD AT DRAWING, OLIVIA.

WHAT ARE YOU DOING?

I THINK IT'S GOING TO HAVE ALL MY FAVORITE THINGS LIKE PINK UNICORNS AND GLITTER RAINBOWS AND HEARTS AND CAT-MERMI-CORNS.

IT'S REALLY ...

PINK.

DO A ROBO MECH WARRIOR!!

ADD MORE LASERS!!

79

84

91

104

105

106

SLAM

132

133

134

149

150

151

153

158

161

181

RING
RING

OKAY, YES, I SEE.
OKAY, THANK YOU.

LIVY? YOUR TEACHER
CALLED. SHE ASKED US
TO COME IN TO
SEE HER.

191

192

197

199

GOODNIGHT, MOM.
GOODNIGHT, BABA.

GOODNIGHT,
NEOI NEOI.

HI, LIVY.

217

PSST LIVY.

YOU THINK SEEING A DOCTOR IS GOING TO HELP YOU?

245

249

Author's Note

Living With Viola is fiction, but this isn't the kind of story you make up out of nowhere. A lot of it is inspired by things that actually happened to me.

My parents were both immigrants to Canada from Hong Kong. As I got older, I saw that immigrants were treated differently, and not always nicely. Other people would make fun of the way they spoke, or think that because they did some things differently it meant they were weird.

But just because something is unfamiliar doesn't mean it's bad or scary. It's important to be open and kind to everyone.

When I was in sixth grade (the same as Livy) I started having panic attacks and feeling nervous and sad all the time. I was sure bad things were going to happen because I was a bad person. I got really good at pretending I was okay on the outside, even while I was terrified on the inside. I didn't understand why I was always so scared.

My parents didn't know what was happening, either. They were very worried for me. They took me to see some doctors, and by the time I was about 16 I was diagnosed with anxiety disorder and panic disorder, with a bit of obsessive-compulsive disorder. Wow! When I finally knew what it was, it felt like the biggest relief. I wasn't alone, and there were things I could do to help me feel better, like cognitive behavioral therapy, medication, group sessions, and talking to people I could trust.

My anxiety didn't exactly exist outside of me the way Viola is with Livy. Often when I was scared, it was like hearing my own voice tell me I was horrible. After getting help, I realized you can't always believe everything you think about yourself. We're not always nice to ourselves, whether or not we have anxiety. But would you say the same things to people you love that you sometimes say to yourself? Thinking about my critical voice as an actual person helped me to say, "Hey, that's pretty mean. Why are you saying these things? They're not true."

When I was a kid, my favorite things to do were to draw and to read. I'm older now but those are STILL my favorite things. I also love pink sparkles and cat unicorn plushies, but I used to worry that liking things that are too "girly" or too "childish" were not cool. I even tried to change, but I didn't find much happiness trying to pretend to like things other people liked. And I realized that there are no girly things, or boyish things, or childish things. There are just things that make you happy.

If you ever feel scared or sad, or don't understand why you feel a certain way, talk to someone about it, like an adult you can trust. There are lots of people like you who understand how you feel and have gone through the same thing. You're not alone!

—Rosena Fung

Cantonese Glossary

 ah ma (a mā): a less formal way of saying mother

 ai yah (ai ya): an exclamation expressing fear, shock, surprise, or dismay

 baba (bā bā): daddy

 bao (bāau): A delicious bun stuffed with meat or sweet fillings like red bean, coconut, or custard. When steamed they are soft and white, when baked they are brown and glazed.

 char siu (chā sīu): sweet red barbecue pork

 cheen chung goh (chīn chàhng gōu): A steamed dessert cake made of egg and custard in alternating layers. Literally translates to "thousand layer cake."

 dim sum (dím sām): Usually eaten during yum cha, dim sum are small shared dishes like dumplings, buns, and other things that don't need to be cut with a knife to be shared by lots of people. They can be sweet or savory, and can be fried, baked, or steamed, often in stackable baskets brought to the table.

 face (mín): Not literally a face! It means how you are perceived by others, having to do with respect or honor in social interactions. Face depends on prestige, roles, reputation, actions, and behaviors. You can "gain face" or "lose face" as a person and it affects how you are seen by others. You can also "give face" to someone with actions that demonstrate respect.

 gah jeh (gā jē): older sister

goong goong (gūng gūng): grandfather, specifically mother's father

 gwoo gwoo (gū gū): aunt, specifically father's sister

 gwaai (gwāai): When pronounced with an upper high intonation, "gwaai" means good or obedient.

 ham yue gai (hàahm ỳuh gāi): salted fish and chicken

 ham yue gai lup chow fan (hàahm ỳuh gāi lāp cháau faahn): salted fish and diced chicken fried rice

 har gow (hā gáau): steamed shrimp dumpling made with a translucent wrapper. Often served together with siu mai.

 joh sun (jóu sàhn): good morning

 lap cheung (laahp chéung): dried red Chinese sausage

 lau sah bao (làuh sā bāau): A dessert made of a steamed white bun full of hot and melting custard, and sometimes a salted egg. Literally translates to "leaking sand bun."

 lei lah (lèih la): A response to being called, like "I'm coming!"

 leng jai (leng jái): a handsome guy, often used to get someone's attention

 leoi (léui): a casual way to say neoi

 lo mai gai (noh máih gāi): sticky rice stuffed with fillings like diced chicken, lap cheung, Chinese black mushroom, salted egg, or shrimp, then steamed in a wrapped in lotus leaf

mah mah (màh màh): When said with a lower intonation, means grandmother, specifically father's mother. (With either an upward or upper high intonation, means mom.)

 maai daan (màaih dāan): a way of asking for the check at the end of a meal

 neoi (néui): Daughter. Neoi neoi (nèuih néui) is also daughter, but more endearing.

 por por (pòh pòh): grandmother, specifically mother's mother

 red packet: Also known as lai see (laih sih), it's a red envelope filled with money given by married couples to younger family members during special occasions like New Year's Day, weddings, graduations, and birthdays.

 siu mai (sīu máai): A dumpling made of steamed pork in an open yellow wrapper. Sometimes includes mushrooms and diced shrimp, and often topped with orange fish eggs.

 sot jor (sōt jó): an unkind and insulting way to talk about someone in reference to their mental health, kind of like saying "crazy"

 yeet hay (yiht hei): In some cultures, certain foods have "cold" energy, and some have "hot" energy (but not necessarily cold or hot in temperature!). If you have too much of one or the other, it will make you feel unwell, and you should eat the other kind of food to get a good balance back. Yeet hay literally translates to "hot air," and can describe "hot" foods (like fries, peanuts, or lychee) or how you feel after eating too much of it.

 yeh yeh: grandfather, specifically father's father

 yum cha (yám chàh): Literally translating to drink tea, yum cha is a tradition of eating out between breakfast and lunchtime where large groups share dim sum and hot tea. Sometimes food is ordered off a list you fill out at the table, while other restaurants have servers push steam-heated carts full of fresh dim sum dishes to choose from.

Character Sketches

Acknowledgments

Living With Viola was created in Toronto/Tkaronto, the traditional territory of the Mississaugas of the Credit, the Anishinaabe, the Chippewa, the Haudenosaunee, and the Wendat peoples. The story of my family's immigration is inextricable from the history of First Nations peoples. I will never forget whose land I'm on, and the histories that are suffused in this ground.

This book could not exist without my extraordinary and sublime editor, Serah-Marie McMahon. Thank you for this journey together and for being my guiding star. Thank you to Annick Press: Katie Hearn, Rick Wilks, Paul Covello, Kaela Cadieux, Heather Davies, Brendan Ouellette, Gayna Theophilus, Asiya Awale, Amanda Olson, and the entire team.

So much love to Mike Rennick and my Deserres fam for being so supportive and for all the laughs. Thank you to the OCADU Illustration faculty team and to my amazing students. To my bff crew Suharu Ogawa, Derrick Chow, Orlando Grünewald, and Hannah Lee—your love and belief in me mean the world. Thank you, Annie Koyama and all my incredible friends, for your endless support.

This book is about family, and this story is the story of my family. Mom, Daddy, Jason Fung and Wendy Wang, and to the future generation of readers—Spencer, Kayleigh, and Luke. I love you all so much. Thank you to Julia and Octavio Medeiros and the entire family. Above all, thank you to my husband, Mark Medeiros, who never stopped believing in this and in me.